Solve it Yourself

The Mystery Squad and the Artful Dodger

Martin Waddell

D1513343

Blackie

British Library Cataloguing in Publication Data
Waddell, Martin
The mystery squad and the artful dodger.
I. Title
823′ .914 [J]   PZ7

ISBN 0-216-91419-1
ISBN 0-216-91418-3 Pbk

The Blackie Publishing Group
Bishopbriggs, Glasgow G64 2NZ
Furnival House, 14/18 High Holborn
London WC1V 6BX

Printed in Great Britain by
Thomson Litho Ltd, East Kilbride, Scotland

Are You a Good Detective?

To solve this case you have to follow the trail wherever it leads you and spot the clues on the way. Some are in the story, some are in the pictures. If you crack the clues first time you get maximum points and end up with a Sherlock Holmes Detective Rating. If you don't, you may find further clues to help you but Beware of Custard Pies!

Add up your points as you go along and check your final score against the Detective Rating Chart on page 95. You'll find out how good you really are!

A book for Dante and Reuben

1

'Careful of that picture, Casey,' Detective-Inspector Peters warned. 'I don't want anything else to happen to it.'

'Is it valuable, Dad?' Casey asked.

We were in Casey's dad's office waiting for him to finish work. He was supposed to be taking us to the speedway at Monks Cross.

'Very!' said Casey's dad. 'It's *Dutch Farm Scene* by an artist called Van Renwick. It's a famous picture. And it nearly put paid to our speedway trip!'

'What happened Mr Peters?' I asked. 'Did somebody steal it?' It didn't look worth stealing to me, just

some mouldy-looking old animals and a barn.

'Somebody *tried* to steal it, Bodger,' said Casey's dad, looking pleased with himself. 'A very clever thief whom we call the Artful Dodger. He wasn't so clever this time! He reckoned without me. Two hours ago, the Artful Dodger had that picture in the back seat of his car, heading out of town . . . straight into one of my road blocks.'

'Road blocks?' said Casey. 'For a *picture*?'

Casey's dad grinned. He flicked open a little book on his desk, and started to read it out loud.

'"Perhaps the finest example of the work of the Master is his *Dutch Farm Scene*. In the picture the colours of field and hedgerow contrast vividly with the sunset, and the composition is marked by the care with which Van Renwick has placed the central figures. The girl and the three men are shown finely grouped, whilst to the left of the picture the two children squabble over scraps as the six white ducklings march majestically by. The three solemn-faced dogs, the stout pigs, and the baby in the girl's arms . . ." It goes on and on, son! Five pages of description of that picture. and but for a smart piece of policework by my men, it could be down at the docks by now, and about to be shipped out of the country.'

'Shouldn't we be going, Dad?' Casey asked. But I wanted to hear more about the Artful Dodger.

'What happened?' I asked.

'The Van Renwick was reported stolen, three hours ago. We slapped on our road blocks at once. Two hours ago we were able to report to the owners that the picture had been recovered, and the thief was in custody.'

'GREAT!' I said, although Casey was making faces at me. He hears a lot about his dad's cases at home, and I suppose he gets fed up with it.

'How was it stolen?' I asked. Being in charge of TSM (Top Secret Material) in the Mystery Squad, I am interested in criminal methods.

'Our friend the Artful Dodger walked into the Broomgrove Gallery, unhooked the picture, and walked out again! Simple. So simple, that nobody stopped him. Typical of the Dodger! They thought he was one of the staff. Of course, now we've got him he denies it. Says he has no idea how the picture got into his car. Knows nothing about the other jobs, either. The Bronze Horse, or the Ching Chessmen. But we've got him, all right, *this* time. He's a real bag of tricks. Swapped a set of plastic chessmen for the seventh-century Ching ivory set . . . and we chased the plastic set for two weeks before we realised what we'd done. Then the Bronze Horse . . . I don't like to think about the Horse! Now this!'

Casey had picked up his dad's book and was looking at a picture in it.

'The Dodger almost had us fooled again. We've been concentrating on the Antiques Fair at the Lower Hall next week. It looked easy meat for our Dodger. What does he do? He turns up *this* week, and walks away with the Van Renwick under his arm.'

'Dad,' said Casey.

'We were quick on the job,' said Casey's dad. 'The police have to be, when a thing like this goes missing.'

'*Dad*!' said Casey. There's something wrong, Dad.'

1

What's wrong?

Casey doesn't want to miss the speedway . . . Turn to section **49**.

Casey has spotted a police procedural flaw . . . Turn to section **17**.

Casey doesn't like the look of the picture . . . Turn to section **31**.

Need a clue? Turn to section **57**.

2

No. Go to **21**.

3

A good answer but the trees are too small to give any help. Turn to **45**.

4

Wrong, go to **20**.

5

Turn to **19**.

6

Wrong. Go to **68**.

7

Wrong. Turn to **62** and think again.

8

Wrong. Turn to **61**.

9

A *good* question, but not the question that *must* be asked. Turn to **28**.

Detective Rating

5 points if you got it right.

Deduct 1 point for each wrong choice.

10

'Our Mr Quirke has just established an alibi,' said Casey. 'He didn't go mad in the park. He knew exactly what he was doing when he chased the ducks, knocked over the painter, and stuck the ice cream cone on that kid's nose.'

'He did odd things which forced people to notice him. And every time he did something he then made a point of asking them the time,' Beans said.

'So they would know where he was, and when he was there?' said James.

'So they would know where he *wasn't*!' said Casey.

'Wasn't?' I blinked at Casey. Now he was going round the twist too!

'Mr Quirke has just made absolutely sure that a lot of people know where he was between one and two o'clock today,' said Casey. 'Which proves he wasn't somewhere else.'

'You mean . . . a crime has been committed between one and two o'clock and he thinks he might be suspected, and so he's making sure he can prove he's innocent?'

'Yes,' said Casey.

'Doesn't work, though, does it?' said James suddenly.

'I think it does,' said Casey, who never likes being contradicted.

What do you think?

If you think James is right, turn to **15**.

If you think Casey is right, turn to **67**.

11

Turn to **36**.

Detective Rating

4 points if you got it straight away.
3 points if you needed a clue.
Deduct 1 point for each wrong answer.

12

'It's the wrong man!' Casey gasped.
   'What?'
   'We're following the wrong person.'
He was right.
The man we were following had a black hat and

coat, and he was carrying a walking stick, but he wasn't Quirke.

'Back to the Lower Hall, quick!' shouted Casey. 'Maybe it *isn't* too late.'

But it was too late. Quirke had gone, and so had Beans.

'Where are they?' said Casey.

Where would you look?

Back in the Lower Hall? Turn to **48**.

In the shops? Turn to **59**.

In the park? Turn to **61**.

Need a clue? Turn to **43**.

Detective Rating

3 points if you decoded the message.

Deduct 1 point if you needed a clue, and 1 for each word you got wrong.

13

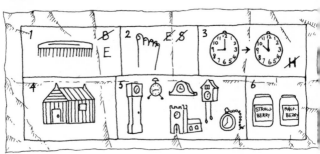

Square 1 = Comb − B = Com + E = *Come*

Square 2 = Toes − ES = To

Square 3 = A clockface, with a moving hand.

           The hand moves through one hour.

           Hour − H = *Our.*

Square 4 = *Shed.*

Square 5 = Six clocks = 6 *o'clock.*

Square 6 = A set of Jam Jars = Jams = *James*

Dead easy!

Casey worked it out, and he arrived down at our shed at six o'clock for the great unveiling!

'This is it!' said James, and he whipped off the cover, actually an old tarpaulin my dad had used for the chip van, which we had before we had the cafe. Our shed is round the back of the cafe.

'Brilliant, isn't it?' I said.

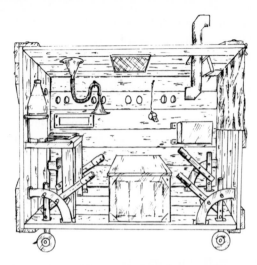

It looked nothing special, just a big wooden crate, with "HANDLE WITH CARE" and "ANTIQUES FOR EXPORT" written on the side in red letters (I did the writing).

'Yeh, great. Great!' said Casey, frowning, but trying to sound enthusiastic at the same time. He never likes to own up that he can't work something out with his Super Detective Brain. He walked round James's Invention admiring it, but he hadn't a clue what it was!

'It's called the Bacon Box, after its Inventor James Bacon MOTMS,' Beans said.

MOTMS means "Member Of The Mystery Squad," so that didn't give Casey any help. James undid the clasp at the side and opened the lid of the box.

'That's the Emergency Ration Box,' I said, pointing it out to Casey with my carrot pen. 'And that's where we'd put the camera.'

'If we had a camera,' James said.

'We have a camera!' said Beans.

'It doesn't work,' said James. He was still cross about the camera. Beans and I used it for underwater photography at the swimming pool.

'It's still a camera,' I said.

'Do we . . . er . . . need a camera?' asked Casey, trying to sound casual. 'I mean what would be the purpose of a camera in this . . . er . . . ?'

James winked at us. Nobody finished Casey's sentence for him. He wasn't going to find out what the Bacon Box was without asking!

'Okay!' Casey groaned. 'I give in. What is it?'

What is the Bacon Box for?

If you think the Bacon Box is a . . .

Mystery Squad Special Operations Box Car . . . Turn to **53**.

Mystery Squad Mobile HQ For Secret Meetings . . . Turn to **30**.

Mystery Squad Mobile Observation Unit . . . Turn to **62**.

Mystery Squad Wooden Tent for All Weather Operations . . . Turn to **70**.

14

This narrows the field a bit for you. Turn to **54**.

15

It doesn't work.
Why not? Turn to **25**.

16

Turn to **55** and think again.

17

Wrong! Turn to **1**.

18

Turn to **36** and try again.

Detective Rating

3 points if you got the right answer straight away.

2 points if you got it after getting a custard-type clue.

Deduct 1 point for each wrong choice.

19

'The mummy!' said Beans. 'The mummy in the mummy case on the Cameron Antiques stall.'

'Rat-Face again,' I said.

"Come off it,' said Casey. 'You wouldn't have a *real* mummy in a mummy case lying open like that.'

'*Exactly*,' said Beans. 'Real mummys are very delicate. They were kept in their airtight cases for centuries. You don't just leave them lying about in public halls, do you?'

'So that isn't a *real* mummy in the case,' I said. 'It's a dummy mummy . . .'

'Or a *person* dressed up as a dummy!' said Beans, bouncing about.

She was right. The police would never have thought of arresting a mummy!

'You'd better tell your dad, Casey!' Beans said.

Casey made a face.

'Go on, Casey,' said James, grinning. 'Tell your dad the thief is in the mummy case, pretending to be a mummy!'

'Supposing Beans is *wrong*?' I said, saying it for Casey.

'I'm not! I'm right!'

'It doesn't sound very likely, does it?' said Casey.

'That's what the Artful Dodger crimes *are* like!'

Beans insisted. 'That's why they work. Quirke and his friends aren't afraid to do the *unlikely* thing. By the time everybody has worked out that the unlikely has happened, they're away!'

'I wish there was some way of proving it, before telling dad,' said Casey.

'Take a look at the mummy,' said Beans.

'Might damage it,' said James. 'If it is real it's fragile.'

'There must be a way,' said Casey.

'There is!' I said, because a BRILLIANT bit had just flashed into my mind.

What did Bodger do?

Close the lid of the mummy case? Turn to **27**.

Stick a pin in the mummy? Turn to **47**.

Punch it? Turn to **40**.

Stand on its toe? Turn to **5**.

Detective Rating

4 points for spotting both without help.
Deduct 1 point for each clue you turned to.
Deduct 1 point for each person you missed.

20

James and Casey and I sped after our quarry, but we had made a terrible mistake!

What was our mistake?

We didn't notice that we were being followed . . .
Turn to **44**.

We let our quarry get too far in front . . . Turn to **4**.

We were following the wrong man . . . Turn to **12**.

If you need a clue, turn to **29**.

21

Right . . . but why?

—So he can plead insanity if caught? Turn to **2**.

—To create an alibi? Turn to **10**.

—To distract people from the fact that he's picking their pockets? Turn to **65**.

22

They'd just escaped from him. He wasn't likely to be helpful! Turn to **45** and try again.

23

Wrong. Go to **25** again.

24

This clue is a load of rubbish. Go to **37**.

Detective Rating

*4 points if you worked out why the alibi didn't work, but
deduct 1 point if you got custard pied!*

25

'Quirke has set out to establish an alibi for a crime
which must have taken place in the last hour, his idea
being to prove that he had nothing to do with it.
Right?' said James.

'That's right,' said Casey. 'A cast iron alibi. He
doesn't want to rely on his friends because the police
might suspect them of lying. He goes around *making*
enemies, knowing that his enemies will remember
what he's done . . . like sticking the ice cream on that
kid's nose. The kid's mum is bound to remember
that. There must be dozens of witnesses who'll
remember what he did in the park.'

'And *when* he did it,' I said.

I couldn't work out what James was on about.

'Witnesses *including* us,' said Beans.

'What does all that *prove*?' asked James.

'It proves he didn't do the crime,' I said.

'The alibi doesn't work!' James insisted. 'Instead
of proving that he has nothing to do with the crime,
his "alibi" proves he must have *something* to do with
it, or he wouldn't know when it was going to
happen!'

'R-I-G-H-T,' said Casey slowly.

'When what was going to happen?' asked Beans.

James shrugged.

'Maybe . . . maybe there has been a hold up at the

Lower Hall and the antique dealers have been robbed!' I said.

'Dry up, Bodge,' said Casey. He was still feeling put out because James had been the one to spot the weakness in the alibi business.

'Supposing Quirke is the leader of an antique stealing gang and they are an international conspiracy and at exactly one-thirty the robbers came in with machine guns and they made all the dealers hand over the best antiques and . . .'

'What gang? What robbers?' said James.

'Quirke's International Antique Stealing Gang,' I said. 'The dreaded QIASG!'

'I thought he was supposed to be a lunatic who was killing people?' grinned James.

'That was before I thought of QIASG!' I said.

'Whichever he is, we'd better get a move on, or we'll lose him!' said Casey.

Quirke was leaving the park, and we belted after him. We didn't have to belt far. He headed straight for the Lower Hall, and reached it just as a familiar typhoon disappeared inside.

'Dad!' groaned Casey. 'He must have heard about this morning.'

But Casey's dad hadn't come to grab Casey. He had come to arrest the Artful Dodger.

'It's Deeny Feeney!' Casey told us, after he'd managed to worm his way through the crowd of anxious dealers.

We looked at each other.

'Deeny?' said James. 'I don't believe it.'

None of us liked Deeny, but that didn't make him the Artful Dodger. For one thing, old Deeny is very stupid!

'The Lower Hall was closed between one and two,' said Casey. 'During that time, Deeny was the only one who was allowed in. He emptied the waste bins and swept the floor. The police checked him going in, and checked him going out again. Nothing. But when the hall was opened up, a lot of stuff had gone missing, including most of the best pieces.'

'That doesn't mean Deeny took them!' Beans protested. We couldn't get over anybody thinking Deeny was the Artful Dodger!

'Deeny had been working in the yard beside the hall, laying cement,' Casey explained. 'Somebody noticed that one bit didn't look as smooth as the rest, and pointed it out to PC Gray. When the wet cement was lifted, there was a bag hidden beneath it with a collection of small objects inside.'

'Doesn't sound like Deeny!'

'Too clever for Deeny!'

'Was the snuff box found?' said James.

We all looked at him.

Casey shook his head. 'I wrote down a list of the stuff,' he said.

'Better give me that,' I said.

'What do you think, Casey?' said James. He was giving the Great Brain a chance to show off again, because Casey had been looking miffed over the alibi business. I have a notion that James had already worked out what the list meant.

'One, the objects are very small,' said Casey. 'Two, they are all metal, and *three . . .*'

'THEY ARE OF VERY LITTLE VALUE!' James and Casey said it together, and grinned at each other.

'Meaning?' said Beans, in bewilderment.

'At least the equivalent of several suitcases full of stuff has gone from the Lower Hall,' said Casey. 'Most of it selected for its value. This lot is worth almost nothing, compared to the other stuff. . . . But it's the worthless stuff which has been recovered.'

'So what?' I said. Casey and James were playing games, and that always annoys me.

'The junk was stolen, but it wasn't meant to *stay* stolen,' said Casey. 'It was meant to be *found*.'

'Why?'

'Why was the forged picture put in the car, the last time the Artful Dodger pulled a job?' said James, breaking in. 'To divert attention away from the real stolen property and the real thief, that's why! The police have found this junk and picked up Deeny Feeney, and by the time they work out that he isn't the Artful Dodger and doesn't know anything about the other missing antiques . . . it will be too late.'

Beans and I just stared at them. We were very impressed. James and Casey make a great team, when they aren't competing with each other.

'Tell your dad!' I said to Casey.

'I will when I can get talking to him,' Casey said. 'He isn't exactly the easiest person in the world to get talking to, when he's working.'

'I reckon Casey's dad will probably work it out for himself,' said James.

'Sure thing,' said Casey.

'But will he do it quickly enough?' said Beans. 'We could tell one of the other policemen . . .'

'We can't really tell anybody anything, until we have some hard evidence,' said James, who is always sensible about that sort of thing. 'All we've got at the moment are theories.'

'Where do we get hard evidence?'

We all thought about it.

Then I had one of my brilliant turns!

'The snuff box!' I gasped.

'What about the snuff box?' Beans said. James and Casey were only half listening to us. They had on their Great Detective Faces and were having a Great Detective Conversation.

'It wasn't with the stuff that was found under the cement.'

'Oh GREAT!' said Beans disgustedly. 'GREAT DETECTIVE WORK, Sherlock Bacon! The snuff box wasn't found. Marvellous . . . except everybody knows that.'

'It *would* have been,' I said, 'it would have been, if I hadn't spotted it being taken this morning from Mr Holden's stall.'

'Is he on about the snuff box again?' said James, suddenly paying us attention. I had mentioned it once or twice when we were in the park, because I was so dead sure I had seen it disappear off Holden's stall.

'Yes, I am,' I said. 'Remember we wondered why Quirke would bother to steal junk like that? Well, the stuff that was found under Deeny's cement was *all* junk.'

'Go on,' said Casey, taking an interest.

'The junk that was put under the cement was put there by someone who meant it to be found. The snuff box was meant to be in that bag. But Quirke couldn't risk using it after he had almost got himself caught, pinching it from Holden's stall. If the snuff box had turned up in the cement, the whole story of what happened this morning might have been looked at again . . . and this time I would have been believed . . . and Mr Quirke would have had a lot of questions to answer.'

'You *could* be right,' said James

Casey looked thoughtful. 'If Quirke planted the stuff under the cement, it must have been before one o'clock, and before the *real* antiques were taken. The whole idea was that the police would start looking when the real theft was discovered. The worthless stuff would be found, putting the police on to the false trail that led them to Deeny Feeney.'

'And by the time the police had worked out that it was just an Artful Dodge, the real criminal would have got away?'

'Right!'

'Quirke got Feeney out of the way somehow, and then he buried the stuff in the cement . . .'

'Quick work,' said Beans.

'Hot work,' said James. 'He wouldn't do that in his overcoat, would he? It would trail in the cement. So he took it off, and we almost missed him because he was in his shirtsleeves.'

'Did he go out to the yard, Beans?' James asked.

Beans nodded. 'I couldn't follow him. There was nowhere for me to hide. I thought if he went out of the yard, you would pick him up.'

'Lovely theories,' said James. 'But still not evidence.'

'If we could prove Quirke was near the cement it might help,' said Casey. 'We'll go and take a look at it, just in case.'

'We won't find a footprint,' James said. 'Quirke is too clever for that.'

We had a look, just the same.

There didn't seem to be much in the way of clues. Scoop marks in the sand. Little rounds holes in the cement. Some twigs sticking up out of the soil in the wheel barrow. Some paint and a paint brush left lying around.

'Don't think much of that lot!' I said.

'You're wrong!' said Casey, confidently. 'There's our proof.'

What's he talking about?

The scoop marks in the sand? Turn to **51**.

The little round holes in the cement? Turn to **35**.

The twigs? Turn to **23**.

The paint things? Turn to **64**.

Detective Rating

3 points if you spotted that the picture was a fake.

Deduct 1 point if you needed a clue, and 1 point for each wrong option you picked. Those with custard pie faces get no points at all.

26

'The art book said that there were six ducks in the picture, and there were only five in the one in your dad's office,' said James. 'That's how you worked out that it was a forgery?'

'Correct!' said Casey, beaming all over his ugly mug.

I was glad he was pleased. I wasn't. For one thing we had missed our Police Complimentary Tickets Trip to the speedway at Monks Cross, and for

another I was getting fed up with hearing How-Casey-Unmasked-The Artful-Dodger's-Forgery. He had already told me several times, and the way Casey told it he got smarter each time. Now we were having an MSM (Mystery Squad Meeting) in the garage at Casey's house, and he was telling it all over again for the benefit of James and Beans.

There are four members of the Mystery Squad. I'm Bodger Bacon and I'm the youngest one. I'm responsible for all TSM (which means Top Secret Material) and record keeping. I keep the TSM in my book, which is the Key to all Mystery Squad Operations. My brother James is our TE (Technical Expert) and my rotten ugly sister Beans is the nutty one. Casey Peters is the Chief of the Mystery Squad because his dad is a detective and Casey knows all about detective methods and solving mysteries. Casey is almost a genius, but he doesn't half go on about it when he gets something right!

'Wait a minute,' my sister Beans said. 'I don't understand. Why did the Artful Dodger steal a forgery? Didn't he know it was one?'

'Punkhead!' I said. 'Of course he knew.'

'Then why did he steal it?'

'He didn't steal it,' said James patiently.

'WHAT?' Beans looked so astonished that we all laughed. 'What was he arrested for, then?'

'He wasn't arrested. That was somebody else. Somebody innocent. Somebody who didn't know anything about the picture, except that it somehow found its way into the back of his car.'

'The man who was arrested wasn't the Artful Dodger?'

'No. But the Dodger put the picture into the back of the car.'

Beans thought about it. 'Why did the Artful Dodger steal a forged picture and put it in the back of someone else's car?' she asked.

'He didn't steal a forged picture,' said Casey. 'He stole a real one. His problem was how to get away, when he knew the police would be alerted at once. He solved it by arranging for a faked picture to be planted in a car heading towards the police road blocks. The picture was discovered, the road blocks called off while my dad sat around congratulating himself . . . and then the Artful Dodger was able to drive out of town, with the *real* picture in his back seat.'

'Bet your dad was angry!' said Beans.

We all know what Casey's dad is like when he gets going.

'That's where we come in,' said Casey.

'US?'

'Yes, us! The Dodger has proved he can outwit the police, but then he's thinking about them, one step ahead all the time. He doesn't even know about us, and he won't be expecting to find the Mystery Squad on his tail, will he?'

'Operation Artful Dodger!' I announced.

'My dad reckons the Artful Dodger still won't be able to resist the big Antiques Fair at the Lower Hall next week,' said Casey. 'Dad'll have the place under observation, of course, but so will we!'

'How?' said James.

'I'm . . . er . . . working on it' said Casey.

'*He's . . . er . . . working on it!*' said James, imitating Casey as we were on our way home. 'In other words the Great Detective likes the idea of doing better than his dad, but hasn't a clue how to set about it.'

'Have you?' I said.

'I'm . . . er . . . working on it,' said James with a grin!

The note was inside Casey's desk after dinner break the next day.

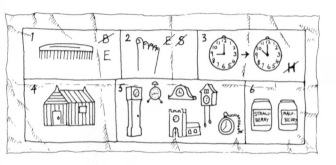

Can you read the message?

If you get it straight away move to **13**.

If you need help turn to **46**.

Detective Rating

4 points if you got it right.

0 points for the custard-pied!

27

I closed the lid on the mummy case!

All I had to do was to wait a minute, until Cameron was out of the way, and then I moved the lid. It settled neatly into position, airtight as it had been for thousands of years.

The mummy wouldn't be able to breathe.

If the mummy was a mummy, that wouldn't matter, because it had given up breathing centuries ago. If it wasn't a mummy . . .

'You did well, kids,' Casey's dad said, as the mummy and Cameron were led away to a waiting police car. 'Too bad we didn't manage to get Quirke as well. . . .I can't figure out what happened to the stolen antiques and these two won't talk.'

'I think Quirke was the brains behind the whole operation, Dad,' said Casey.

'How did you get on to him in the first place?' said Casey's dad.

'It was Bodge!' Casey said. 'He was hiding in our Mystery Squad Observation Unit.'

'Your *what?*' said his dad.

Casey looked uncomfortable.

'We wanted to stake the place out, Dad. We had to have somewhere to hide. James and Bodger and Beans thought up this box, that would look like a crate for holding antiques . . .'

'. . . and we put it on the stage, with the other crates,' said James.

'Beans and I did, and I did the hiding,' I said quickly.

'Let me see,' said Casey's dad.

We showed him the crates.

'That's our one,' I said, lifting up the flap.

'Bit of a mess, isn't it?' he said.

Our Mystery Squad Observation Unit was full of rubbish!

'Deeny Feeney!' said Casey. 'I bet he was too lazy to go to the rubbish bins at lunch-time. That's how he was so quick. He dumped his rubbish in our crate!'

'My pen!' I said.

'What?'

'It's my carrot pen. The one Beans bust.'

'So?'

'Don't you see?' I said. 'It's solved. I've solved the Locked Room Mystery . . . I know how the thief got the stolen things out of the Hall.'

How was it done?

The main door was locked on the inside, and the side doors were bolted on the inside. The police were in their positions. (See map in **68**). How did the thief, dressed as a mummy, get the stolen antiques out of the hall?

Turn to **37** if you've worked it out.

If you need a clue, turn to **24**.

Detective Rating

6 points if you spotted the small object being stolen.

Deduct 1 point if you needed a clue, and 1 point for each incorrect option you chose.

28

I showed the Dodger's hat trick, which was very simple. He went to the stall, with his hat in his hand. He placed the hat on the edge of the stall, being careful to place it on top of a small object. When he lifted the hat, the object was gone!

'I think he flipped it off the end of the stall, into that bag!' I said.

'This is an outrage!' barked the man with the stick.

Casey and James had been quick as lightning. It is in situations like these that Casey being Casey *Peters* helps, because having a dad who is a detective-inspector means that the police take you seriously. Casey had got the policeman from the end of the hall, in double quick time.

'This man is the Dodger!' I said. 'I can prove it.'

'But that bag belongs to me!' said Mr Holden, the old guy who owns the stall.

My jaw dropped open.

'This is ridiculous!' snapped the man with the stick. He had gone purple in the face.

A rat-faced guy from the Cameron Antiques Stall came up and started shouting about the man with the stick being Mr Quirke, of Quirke and Quirke Antiques.

'Mr Quirke is a major exporter of antiques, Officer,' said Mr Holden.

'He's the Dodger!' I said. 'Exporting antiques is exactly what he does . . . stolen antiques.'

The policeman frowned at me.

'Officer,' said Mr Quirke, 'perhaps you would like to calm this child down by searching through the bag.'

I saw James glance at Casey. Casey was looking sick. They thought I had picked the wrong man, but I hadn't. I had got the right man, and he was trying to bluff his way out.

'Go on, search it!' I said, though I had no idea why he should be knocking things into Mr Holden's bag.

There was nothing in the bag.

'What about his hat?' I demanded desperately.

'Dry up, Bodge,' said James.

Mr Quirke twirled his hat under our eyes. There was obviously nothing in it.

'Search him!' I said. 'I know he has it on him somewhere.'

'Er . . . um . . .' said Casey.

'I think an apology would be in order, don't you?' said the policeman.

'He's . . . er . . . very sorry, sir,' said James, glowering at me.

'He's an idiot,' muttered Casey, glumly.

'So be it!' said Quirke, and he turned on his heel and stalked off, with his black hat set firmly on his head.

The policeman looked down his nose at Casey. 'You know the score, don't you, son?' he said. 'If Mr Quirke lodges an official complaint about this incident . . .'

'Dad isn't going to be pleased!' said Casey.

'You're right there!' said the policeman, and he walked back to his station by the door.

'You'll get Casey into trouble with his dad, Bodge!' snapped Beans. 'You *nit*!'

'Doesn't matter, Bodge,' Casey said, trying to look cheerful. Casey's dad isn't very happy about there being a Mystery Squad at all, even though we have helped him out a few times. He's always afraid that Casey will get into real trouble.

'There's just one detail we ought to check out first,' said James, suddenly. 'You wouldn't be the only one in trouble, Casey, if the story got back to your dad.'

'He means *us*,' said Beans, pulling a face. 'We'd be in BIG trouble.'

'I mean the policeman,' said James.

'What?'

'The unasked question!' said James. 'I bet Casey's dad wouldn't be pleased if he knew about a detail like that being missed.'

What is the unasked question?

Ask the door-keeper if he has seen anyone acting suspiciously? Turn to **9**.

Ask Mr Holden if any of his stock is missing? Turn to **54**.

Ask Mr Quirke to allow a body search? Turn to **66**.

Ask if anyone has seen the Artful Dodger? Turn to **69**.

29

Turn to **20**.

30

Nor a Mobile HQ. Only room for one person inside!
Reconsider the options in **13**.

31

Right! But why not? Check the pictures in **1**.
Move to **26** when you've sussed it out.

32

Wrong. Go to **68**.

33

Wrong. Turn to **62** and think again.

34

Wrong. Turn to **61**.

Detective Rating

3 points if you spotted it straight away.
Deduct 1 point for each mistake you made.

35

'That mark was made by the tip of Quirke's walking stick when he planted the things under the cement,' said Casey.

'Which means *before one o'clock*,' said James. 'He left here at one, we know that. The trouble is, we have no means of proving that he didn't make that mark *after two*, when he came back here, *after* the things had been recovered.'

'I think we can prove it,' said Casey. 'Take a closer look at the print in the cement.'

'I know!' I said. 'It's had time to harden, hasn't it? Which means it has been there quite a long time . . .'

'It's still squishy!' said Beans.

'Cement doesn't harden all that quickly,' said James. 'What do you mean, Casey?'

'You see there are *two* rings making up the tip mark, an inner one and an outer one,' said Casey.

'What does that tell you?'

I hadn't a clue, and neither had Beans. James was a long time answering, but in the end he got it.

'The tip of Mr Quirke's stick has been damaged,' he said. 'It's hollow. The outer ring is the circle made by the shape of the stick itself, the inner one is the shape of the hole.'

'Right!' said Casey, sounding very pleased with himself. 'Quite a deep hole in the tip, too!'

'So?'

'So we can use Mr Quirke's funny alibi business in the park to prove that he visited Deeny Feeney's cement bed *before* one o'clock!'

We all stood there gaping at him!

'Get a straw and poke it in the hole, Bodge,' said Casey.

'Eh?' I said.

'I'm serious,' said Casey. 'It ought to provide us with the evidence we need.'

How?

If you understand how turn to 55.

If you need help turn to 63.

Detective Rating

If you spotted that the playground tower would be the best look-out post, straight away, you score 4 points. Deduct 1 point for each wrong answer.

36

We went to the adventure playground, and up on to the high tower, where we had the best view possible of the whole park.

'There they are!' said James.

'Has he gone mad?' I said.

Mr Quirke was bouncing around angrily, wagging his stick at a man who looked as if he was a painter. Somebody had knocked the painter off his ladder. There was paint everywhere, and the painter was obviously shouting back at Quirke, although they

were too far away for us to make out what they were saying.

'There's Beans!' said Casey. 'Come on, we'd better get over there.'

We scrambled down the tower . . . at least, they did. I used the swing rope. They don't call me Tarzan Bacon for nothing. It was EET (Emergency Escape Training).

By the time we'd caught up with Beans, Mr Quirke had given up arguing with the painter and gone to sit on a bench.

'What was all that about?' Casey asked.

Beans was looking puzzled.

'I don't know,' she said. 'Maybe he's funny in the head, or something. He walked up to that man and kicked his ladder. The man fell off and the paint went all over the place, and Quirke laughed at him. Then they started to argue.'

'Uh?' said James.

'That's not the only thing he's done, either,' said Beans. 'He flicked mud at the ducks with his stick and shouted at them. The park keeper had to come up and stop him. People were complaining.'

'He *is* mad!' I said.

'He's certainly *acting* mad,' said James.

'Maybe he isn't the Artful Dodger after all,' I said. 'Maybe he is a dangerous criminal who has escaped from a lunatic asylum and killed the real Mr Quirke and now he is reaching breaking point and he's going to start killing people and . . .'

'Looks just like a man on a bench to me,' said Casey.

'In between doing mad things, he sits there and checks his watch,' said Beans. 'He keeps looking at it, and asking people the time.'

'I bet he's waiting for his fence, so that he can pass on the stolen snuff box!' I said.

'You said he was an escaped lunatic,' James said, grinning.

'He's pretending to be an escaped lunatic, so that no one will realise he is the Artful Dodger,' I said. 'He's waiting for his boss to turn up so that he can hand over the snuff box.'

'Here comes the boss!' said James cheerfully.

It wasn't the boss. It was a little kid on a tricycle in a cowboy hat. The little kid rode right up to Quirke and stood looking at him. The kid was licking an ice cream.

'I bet the kid is an international crook, and the ice cream is a microphone made to look like an ice cream, so he can send messages back to base!' I said.

'Bit small for an international crook!' said Beans. Then . . . 'OH!' she gasped.

'Look at that!' said James, in amazement.

Quirke had reached out his hand and taken the ice cream from the kid. Then, suddenly, he poked the ice cream towards the kid's nose. It stuck there, and the kid began to yell! The kid was dripping ice cream and his mother came up. She started shouting at Quirke and Quirke shouted back.

'He did that on purpose!' I said in amazement.

Finally, Quirke and the kid's mum stopped shouting. Quirke made it up with the kid and bought him another ice cream. Quirke looked at his watch and said something, and the woman looked at hers, and then Quirke seemed to alter his. He raised his hat politely to them and went off, leaving the kid's mother gazing after him, a puzzled look on her face.

It was nothing to the puzzled look that was on mine.

'Come on,' said Casey. 'After him!'

'I'm not sure I want to go after him,' I said. 'I think he *is* mad. Mad as a hatter! I don't fancy getting mixed up with mad people.'

'Not mad,' said Casey. 'Just trying to be clever.'

'He stuck that ice cream on the kid's nose, Casey!'

'I know,' said Casey. 'I saw him do it.'

'But . . . but why should he? And why did he knock that man off the ladder? And why did he chase the ducks?'

'Beats me,' said James, shrugging his shoulders.

'I think I've got it!' said Beans. 'It's to do with the watch, isn't it?'

'Right!' Casey said.

James looked cross.

'Do you mean . . . his watch is STOLEN?' I said.

Casey shook his head.

'It's an old trick,' he said. 'You saw him showing the kid's mum his watch, didn't you?'

'I'll bet he was complaining about being late for an urgent appointment,' said Beans.

'But he couldn't be . . . he's been waiting about in here for ages, and he's kept on checking the time.'

'Exactly,' said Casey.

What is Quirke up to?

He's gone mad. Turn to 11.

He's waiting for his boss. Turn to 18.

He's pretending to be mad. Turn to 21.

His watch has gone wrong and he's checking the time. Turn to 58.

Detective Rating

5 points if you got it first time.
3 points if you needed a clue.

37

'The rubbish bins!' said Casey's dad. 'Clever!'

'It got round the Locked Room problem,' said Casey. 'The thief dressed as the mummy got out of the case when the Hall was empty, unbolted the door leading to the bin area, and brought the bins *in*, one by one, dumping their contents in the crates that were on the stage. He filled them with the stolen

antiques, and put the bins back out again. Then re-bolted the door, and got back into his hiding place.'

'With my policemen standing not twenty yards away at the end of the alley, admiring the view,' said Casey's dad. 'Good thing you kids got on to it.'

We had a feeling *somebody* was going to be in trouble. I felt sorry for those policemen. They couldn't see the bins from the end of the alley, so it wasn't really their fault.

'The Artful Dodger strikes again!' said Casey.

'His Artful Dodge was an extra twist this time,' said James.

'Huh?'

'The Artful Dodges have all been to draw attention away from the real crime, haven't they? By the time the Dodge has been discovered, the criminal has got away. This time, it wasn't like that. The criminal was still here, and so was the stuff he was stealing, but because the Dodge had been discovered, we all *thought* the crime was over. Two Dodges, for the price of one.'

'It isn't over yet,' said Casey's dad.

'Quirke?' said Casey.

'Right,' said Casey's dad. 'I expect your Mr Quirke will be arriving shortly in something which will look very like a bin lorry. He's in for a surprise when he gets here!'

'Which *we* want to see,' said the whole Mystery Squad!

Casey's dad got us a safe position, in an office just across the road from the Lower Hall, with windows overlooking the alley. That way, even if things went wrong, we couldn't get into trouble.

It was nearly six o'clock before Quirke showed up. He wasn't looking like the smart Mr Quirke we knew at all. He was dressed in overalls, like a bin man, with a squashy cap pulled down over his ears.

He pulled up outside the back of the hall, and got out of the lorry cab. Then he strolled, whistling, down the alley.

Casey's dad let him get so far, and no further.

That's how we cracked the Mystery!

Casey even managed to get hold of a Special Souvenir for my TSM Museum.

'That's why all the things which Quirke took were small, and contained metal,' James explained. 'What he did was to place his hat over them, and then they were pulled up inside the hat by the magnet hidden in the crown . . . not knocked off the table into a bag, as Bodger thought.'

'But . . . we saw inside the hat!' I said.

'Watch this!' said Casey.

'Once the object was attracted up into the top of the hat by the magnet, Quirke pulled at the hat band with his finger, and that tightened the mouth of the upside down "bag" into which the stolen object had been drawn by the magnet!' Casey explained. 'Then he could flash the inside of his hat at us all as much as he wanted to, because it *looked* as if it was empty.'

'Great!' I said.

'Another Artful Dodge!' said James, looking at the hat. 'I reckon I could improve on this, though. What if . . .'

'No, James!'

'Leave it, James!'

'Forget it!'

We all spoke at once. We'd had quite enough of
Artful Dodges.

'But . . .'

'Save your energy for the next Mystery, James,'
Casey told him.

He did . . . and we did!

**Now look at the Detective Rating Chart on p. 95
and find out how good a Detective you are!**

38

Ask your mum!

Go to **68**.

39

This narrows the field a bit for you. Turn to **54**.

40

Turn to **19**.

41

Wrong. Turn to **45**.

42

Wrong. Turn to **62** and think again.

43

Turn to **12**.

44

Wrong, go to **20**.

Detective Rating

3 points if you got it straight away.
1 point if you needed a second go.

45

Beans had taken the drinks tins from the container beside the stall at the park gates, and put them down at regular intervals across the grass.

We ran as hard as we could along the path she had laid, up the hill and then . . .

'Oh no!' breathed Casey. 'He's picked up the trail.'

'Hey, Mister!' I shouted. 'Hey! Those are our tins!'

'Oh, they are, are they! Litterbugs!'

The next minute we were in full flight, with the park keeper coming after us, shouting and yelling about people messing up his park with drink cans.

'You idiot, Bodge!' Casey shouted, as we dodged down among the trees.

Luckily for us, the park keeper soon gave up. He went back towards the drink stall, still carrying the tin cans which Beans had meant as a trail for us to follow, and looking very angry.

We waited until he was well out of the way, and then came out from behind the bushes.

'Now we've really lost Beans!' I said. 'Imagine that rotten parkee picking up her trail!'

'What do we do?'

We thought about it.

'The best thing is to split up and each cover one of the exits,' Casey suggested. 'There's the one by the canal, the one by the hospital, and the one at Ziggars . . .'

'And the one we came in by,' said James. 'That makes *four*.'

'There are only three of us!' I said.

'She could be anywhere in the park,' James said. 'Wherever Quirke has gone, Beans will be following, expecting us to come after her.'

'I know what we need,' I said.

'What?' said the other two.

'A helicopter,' I said. 'If we had a helicopter we could swoop over the park and spot them and . . .'

'SHUT UP, BODGE!'

'It's a good idea,' I said. 'Except we haven't got a helicopter, have we?'

'No.'

'Maybe Beans will signal to us.'

'Oh yes? How is she supposed to find where *we* are?' said James.

'We should carry flares,' I said. 'Then if we get lost on an operation we could fire a flare off.'

Nobody said anything.

'I think it's a brilliant idea,' I said. 'I'm going to put it in my TSM book.' My TSM book is where I keep a record of Top Secret Material.

'If we had water pistols filled with dye we could squirt them at trees and make marks for trailing that way,' I said. 'I think that's an even better idea, don't you?'

'ONE' said Casey.

'TWO' said James.

'T-H-R-E-E!' said Casey.

'Get him!' shouted James.

It was rotten! They were both after me.

'Hey! HEY, STOP IT!' I shouted, and then James thudded into me and I went over. 'STOP IT. STOP! What about Beans? What about Beans and Quirke?'

That stopped them.

'We'll get you later.'

'And if you don't stop talking we'll get you *twice*!' Casey said.

'You shouldn't be thumping me,' I said. 'You should be concentrating on finding Beans before Quirke pulls one of his Artful Dodges!'

'There must be a way of spotting where they are, even if we can't lay hands on Bodger's helicopter,' James said.

Then Casey said . . .

What did Casey say?

'I'm fed up and I'm going home!' Turn to **41**.

'Bodge, climb a tree.' Turn to **3**.

'Let's go to the tower in the adventure playground.' Turn to **36**.

'Why don't we ask the park keeper where the trail of tins led to?' Turn to **22**.

'We'll spread out and cover as much ground as we can, in the hope of spotting Beans or Quirke.' Turn to **52**.

46

Cross out "B"

Replace it with "E"

= COME

Turn to **26** and solve the rest.

47

Wrong. Turn to **27**.

48

Wrong. Turn to **12** again.

49

Custard Pie Splatt. You forgot to *duck* and you've collected a face full of custard pie. Go to **1** and think again.

50

In the bag?
Turn to **62** and reconsider the options.

51

Wrong. Go to **25** again.

52

Too hit and miss. Turn to **45** and try again.

53

No steering. No pedals. Not a Box Car.
Go to **13** and think again.

Detective Rating

3 points, deduct 1 for each wrong option you chose . . .
but you get NO points if you were custard pied!

54

'Anything missing, Mr Holden?' James asked the old
man.

The crime we suspected was theft, and the vital
and unasked question was what, if anything, was
missing.

'It was a sn . . .' I started to say, but Casey shot me
a look that shut me up.

Mr Holden blinked at James over the top of his
glasses. He knows James well, because sometimes he
comes across old clocks, and James is good with
clocks.

'My brother thought that something had been
stolen from your stall, Mr Holden,' James said,
prompting the old man.

The trouble is, Mr Holden is very old. He didn't
seem to be certain whether anything was missing or
not.

'It was a snuff box, Mr Holden!' I burst out.
'There was a snuff box at the end of your stall. That
man Quirke took it. He is the Dodger!'

'So you say!' said Beans, sounding as if she didn't
believe me. 'You're always seeing things and imagin-
ing big crime conspiracies. You know you are.'

'I didn't imagine this one!' I flared up.

'Mr Holden?' said James, gently.

'Can't be sure, James. Can't be sure,' said Mr
Holden. 'Been busy, you know. I'd have to check my

records. Difficult to say . . .' he went on mumbling.

'I think he doesn't know for sure what he's got!' said James, when we had left the old man. 'Poor old Holden. Quirke picked his victim well.'

'If there is a victim. If anything was stolen,' said Casey.

'Bodger's imagination!' said Beans.

'It wasn't!' I insisted.

'What *exactly* did you see, Bodger?' said Casey.

I told him, exactly.

'So you didn't see the snuff box being dropped into the bag?'

I shook my head.

'If Quirke is the Artful Dodger, he must have hidden it somewhere else,' said Casey.

There was a pause.

'If he is the Artful Dodger, why is he going round pinching snuff boxes?' said James. 'He's in the big league, isn't he? Pictures worth hundreds of thousands. Not snuff boxes.'

'Perhaps it was a very *valuable* snuff box?' said Beans.

James shook his head. 'If it had been valuable, Mr Holden would have known all about it. He may be getting on a bit, but he still remembers his good stock. It's the junk he isn't able to remember.'

'Why pinch something small, that isn't worth much?' said Casey, beginning to get interested.

'Maybe he's up to an Artful Dodge!' said Beans.

She meant it as a joke, but Casey didn't seem to take it that way.

'*If* Bodge is right, and the snuff box vanished after Quirke was nosing round the stall, then he *must* have a *reason* for taking it. He's a big dealer, he would

never risk taking a small thing like that for nothing.
It isn't in the bag, and it isn't on the stall.
Conclusion?'

'He still has it on him!' said James.

'And he intends doing something with it!' said Casey.

'So?'

'The snuff box was there, according to Bodge, and then it wasn't. Quirke must be up to some artful dodge with it. Therefore what do we, as the Mystery Squad, do?'

Trust Casey to get us going again! It was obvious. We had to concentrate on trailing Quirke, to see what he was up to.

'We'll tail him!' I said. 'Operation Dodger's Footsteps!'

When we started off as the Mystery Squad Casey showed us lots of tailing techniques. All the practice we did then had to come in handy sometime, and this was one of the occasions.

We didn't all hang about inside the Lower Hall as a group, waiting to go dashing off up the street after Quirke when he came out.

Beans stayed in the hall, because she hadn't been much involved in the row with the policeman, and Quirke was least likely to recognise her. The rest of us took up positions outside, with each of us appearing to be *doing* something. Casey says that "doing something" is an important tailing technique, because nothing is more obvious than someone who is just "watching".

We remained alert for a tall, bowler-hatted figure leaving the Lower Hall, complete with black coat and stick.

When he came out, we moved after him. Quietly, quickly and professionally, the Mystery Squad went into action.

Can you spot James and Bodger?

If you can spot James and Bodger without help turn to **20**.

If you can't spot Bodger, turn to **39**.

If you can't spot James, turn to **56**.

If you can't spot Casey, turn to **14**.

Detective Rating

6 points if you got it straight off.
4 points if you needed a clue.

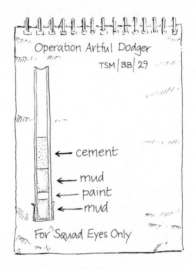

Operation Artful Dodger

TSM | BB | 29

← cement
← mud
← paint
← mud

For Squad Eyes Only

This is an exhibit from my TSM.

You can see the different layers of stuff that got caught in the hollow tip of Quirke's stick.

First there was the cement, which was damp and gooey. When Quirke flicked mud at the ducks, some of it stuck to the cement. Then he knocked over the painter, and the white paint stuck to the mud, and after that more mud stuck to the white paint.

I reckon it was a master stroke of Casey's to think of it.

It meant we could *prove* that Quirke had been messing about round the cement *before* he went to the park at one o'clock.

Casey's straw method was a work of genius.

It was a very quick operation.

It had to be!

First, Beans barged into Quirke.

She gave him a really good barge. His hat went one way, his stick went another, and he almost went over himself.

Beans started apologising and carrying on about how upset she was, and at the same moment James and Casey closed in on him.

It didn't take me a second to push the plastic straw into the hollow tip of the stick, although I almost lost it as Quirke grabbed his property.

Then he recognised us.

'You!' he growled.

'Scarper!' shouted Casey.

And we did.

It didn't matter. We'd got what we wanted!

'Now what?' said Beans, who was all excited because her bit had turned out well.

'The first thing is to get Deeny Feeney off the hook,' said James.

'We'd better tell Dad,' said Casey.

It was the right idea, but telling Casey's dad something in the middle of an investigation isn't always easy. When we finally got to him he was shouting down the telephone.

'. . . and a search round the docks area. This stuff is worth a fortune. Now the Dodger has nicked it, we've got to stop him getting it out of the country.'

He cupped his hand over the telephone.

'What is it, Casey?'

'Er, Dad,' Casey began. 'Deeny Feeney . . .'

'WHAT?' Casey's dad shouted down the telephone. 'Listen, I . . . hold on a minute, will you, somebody's trying to tell me something.'

'Dad, Deeny Feeney isn't the Artful Dodger,' said Casey.

'HOLD ON . . . HOLD ON A MINUTE.' He was still shouting down the telephone. 'HOLD ON.' Then he spoke to Casey. 'I know *that* Casey. What do you think I am? Deeny Feeney couldn't steal a marble from his granny. WHAT? LOOK—DO IT! OKAY?' Casey's dad had gone back to yelling down the telephone. He waved a dismissive hand at us.

'Quirke . . .' Casey began.

'YES. THAT'S WHAT I SAID!'

'He's got an alibi, Dad, only . . .'

'Casey,' said his dad, 'I don't care who has an alibi! The Artful Dodger has done it again. He's made a fool of me. I'm the one who needs an alibi, Casey . . . an alibi to show I wasn't in charge of this shambles!

WHO? YES. AND PC ANDREWS. The main thing I need now is the stuff that was stolen, got that? I'm setting up raids on every person or place I can think of . . . and right now I haven't got time to discuss anybody with or without an alibi . . . not till I get that stuff. So go away!'

Casey backed off.

I thought I would show Casey's dad my straw. I thought if I showed him my straw he would understand.

'O-U-T—OUT!'

I never heard Casey's dad yell like that before!

We all got out.

'We tried,' Casey said.

'Yes, we did,' said James.

'We'll try again, later,' said Casey.

'With bricks, as well as straw!' said James, with a grin.

'What bricks?' said Beans.

'You can't make bricks without straw,' James explained. 'It's a saying. In our case, it means we can't prove anything without a lot more evidence . . . more than Bodger's straw, anyway.'

I didn't say a thing. My straw was a bit bent, but Casey's dad hadn't disturbed the evidence, because I had taped over the ends of the straw with sellotape.

'One thing I noticed,' said James. 'We know more about the Artful Dodger than your dad does, Casey.'

'What do you mean?'

'Your dad is quite wrong about the Dodger.'

'Casey's dad didn't say anything about the Dodger, James,' I said.

'Your dad keeps talking about the Artful Dodger crimes as though they were being committed by one man,' said James. 'He keeps saying "He" did this and "He" did that. But we know there is a team involved.'

'Do we?' I said.

'There must be at least two of them,' said James. 'We know that Quirke wasn't at the Lower Hall between one and two o'clock when the antiques disappeared, so he can't have taken them. But at the same time we reckon he set up the "Artful Dodge" with the junk hidden in the cement that was supposed to make the police suspect Deeny Feeney. That means at least two of them, doesn't it?'

'Three,' said Casey.

Who is right?

Casey? Turn to **68**.

James? Turn to **71**.

Neither of them? Turn to **16**.

56

This narrows the field a bit for you. Turn to **54**.

57

This calls for Quack Thinking!
Turn to **1** and try again.

58

Wrong. Turn to **36** and try again.

59

Wrong. Turn to **12** again.

60

Wrong. Go to **68**.

Detective Rating

If you went to the park straight away 3 points.

If you needed a clue first, 2 points.

Deduct 1 point for each wrong answer.

61

Beans had done brilliantly at the Lower Hall when she put her baseball hat over the "-ING" on the "NO PARKING" sign so that we were left to spot the word "PARK" with Beans's hat beside it . . . almost as good as writing her name on it.

She wasn't the only brilliant one. I reckoned the person who spotted it was brilliant too, but I am too modest to say who that was.

The person-who-spotted-it-who-shall-be-nameless was busy congratulating himself as we arrived at the park gates, where he got a nasty shock.

'Okay, Bodge,' said James. 'You are the genius at spotting Beans's clues. Which way has she gone this time?'

Beans and I have practised laying trails a lot together, working on ways to tell each other where to go next, so naturally James asked me.

'That way!' I said, and I showed them how Beans had done it. Again!

How had Beans laid the trail?

The sticks? Turn to **34**.

The glove? Turn to **8**.

The beer cans? Turn to **45**.

Detective Rating

4 points for the right answer but deduct 1 point for each wrong option you selected.

62

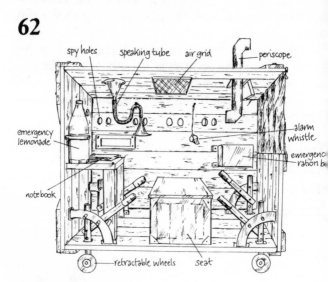

'It's the Mystery Squad Mobile Observation Unit!' said James.

'Like a bird-watcher's hide,' I said. 'Bird-watchers stick bits of branches and leaves on, to make their hides look like the countryside.'

'We're supposed to be a Mystery Squad, not bird-watchers,' said Casey snootily.

'For Artful-Dodger spotting!' I said.

Casey's face cleared. He had got it at last! The Great Brain creaked into operation!

'We put it on the stage in the Lower Hall with all the other packing cases and equipment,' he said. 'Then we spy on the Antiques Fair?'

'That's it,' said James. 'It will look like one of the dealers' crates. That's what the signs on the side are for . . . in place of the bird-watcher's leaves and branches.'

'And I hide inside and when I see the Dodger getting ready to steal something I blow my whistle and jump out through the escape route at the back, where the canvas flap is. You and James have to collar the Dodger.'

'Why *you* in the box, Bodge?' asked Casey. I bet he fancied being the Bacon Box Spy himself.

'Because he's the only one small enough to hide inside,' said Beans. 'Anyway, it means we won't have to look at his rotten face.'

'Not bad, is it?' I said, ignoring her.

'It's brilliant!' said Beans.

We all knew Casey thought it was brilliant too, but he didn't want to say so, because the Bacons had made the Bacon Box all by themselves, without Super Brain, who hadn't even been able to work out what it was for!

'There's just one catch,' said James. 'How are we going to get it into the Lower Hall?'

'That's what the wheels are for,' I said, puzzled. 'We wheel it in, like you said.'

'They aren't going to let us wheel it in, Bodge,' said James.

'Casey's dad . . .' my voice faded away. Casey's dad would go bananas if he thought we were interfering. It would be all right if we caught the Dodger, but nobody fancied telling Casey's dad what we were up to beforehand.

'Don't worry,' Casey said, sounding very casual. 'I think I have a plan that will get round the problem.'

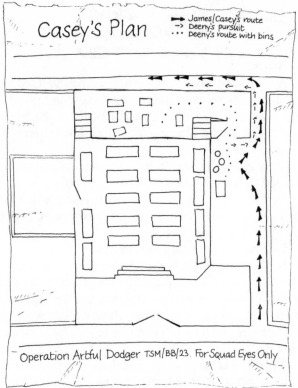

Casey's Plan

→ James/Casey's route
⇢ Deeny's pursuit
⋯ Deeny's route with bins

Operation Artful Dodger TSM/BB/23. For Squad Eyes Only

It was 0845 hours.

Beans and I crouched in the alley beside the Lower Hall, behind the Bacon Box, otherwise known as the Mystery Squad Mobile Observation Unit, which was pretending to be just-a-crate!

The Casey Plan was about to go into action. If everything worked out we would be inside the Lower Hall with the Bacon Box on the stage with the other crates, and no one any the wiser.

There was a creaking sound, as the bolts of the hall side door were opened from the inside.

'Here he comes!' hissed Beans. She was eating an orange from the emergency rations, and she almost choked on it in excitement! Serve her right. The emergency rations were meant for the Bacon Box Spy, not his fat-faced assistant.

I gave a soft "peep" on my whistle.

It was the "Get ready" signal for Casey and James, who were waiting at the High Street end of the alley, all muffled up in anoraks and scarves so that Deeny Feeney wouldn't recognise them.

Deeny Feeney is the odd-job man at the Lower Hall. He is a thin guy with arms like an octopus. He goes around spitting at people and picking his nose. Making an idiot of Deeny Feeney was one of the nicer bits of Casey's plan.

The back door of the hall opened, and Deeny came out, lugging his rubbish bins after him. He had three of them, and he dumped them with a great crash.

I blew my whistle, loudly this time.

Deeny jumped.

James and Casey came charging down the alley at him, yelling and waving their arms about. Deeny gaped at them, and stepped back as they went barging by. He didn't move until they were past him, and then he realised what had happened.

Casey and James had grabbed a bin lid each as they sped past the bins.

'Hey, you!' Deeny shouted, as James and Casey disappeared round the corner into the High Street. Then he was off in hot pursuit, leaving the side door of the Lower Hall open behind him.

'Let's go!' Beans shouted and she jumped up and bounced all over me to get at the Bacon Box.

'Hey!' I said.

Beans had bounced all over my carrot pen, and crushed it.

'What am I going to make notes with now?' I said bitterly. It is just like my elephant-sister to stand on my carrot pen in mid-operation.

'Use a pencil,' said Beans and she scooped my bust carrot pen up and dropped it in the bin.

'Thanks a lot!' I said.

'Just disposing of the evidence,' said Beans.

We had oiled the wheels of the Bacon Box, so that it rolled easily. We got it through the door and up on to the stage in the Lower Hall, long before Deeny Feeney came back with his bin lids. James and Casey had dropped them according to plan, when they reckoned we had had all the time we needed.

'In you get, Bodger!' Beans said.

I slipped through the canvas escape hatch at the back of the box (James had insisted on it, for safety reasons. He said it was too risky to get inside a box, even if it had catches on the inside. So we had removed a section along the top edge of the box, and covered it with a canvas flap).

Casey's plan was an A1 success.

Now it was all up to the Bacon Box Spy, Bodger Bacon!

GREAT!

By the time the Fair got going, it didn't seem so great!

You try sitting all cramped up inside a Mystery Squad Mobile Observation Unit for hours. I knew now why everyone had been so quick to agree to my doing it!

I ate all the emergency rations and most of the sweets and I got a sore foot from sitting on it, and all the time I was watching people through the spy holes.

James and Casey took up their positions where they could keep a good eye on the Box, and Beans stayed close to the door.

We thought that standing staring at people would do no good, because the Artful Dodger wouldn't try to steal something with everyone staring at him.

I looked and I looked until I was really fed up, and in the end I almost missed what I was looking for.

But I didn't!

Had I seen what I *thought* I'd seen?

I couldn't see enough to be certain from inside the box. There was only one thing for it. I poked my head through the canvas flap, to get a full view.

One look was enough. I blew my whistle!

What crime does Bodger think is being committed?

A pocket is being picked? Turn to **72**.

Money is being stolen? Turn to **42**.

A goblet's being grabbed? Turn to **33**.

A very large object has been removed? Turn to **7**.

A small object is being taken? Turn to **28**.

Need a clue? Turn to **50**.

63

The cement was wet. There was mud in the park.
There was white paint, dropped on top of the mud.
The tip of the stick was hollow. Turn to **55**.

64

Wrong. Go to **25** again.

65

No. Go to **21**.

66

Reasonable . . . but there's one question which comes
first. Turn to **28**.

67

You're wrong!

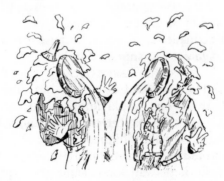

Go to **15**.

Detective Rating

3 points if you got it straight away.

2 points if you got it after one mistake.

68

'Someone had to make sure that the police discovered the stuff that was hidden under the cement,' said Casey. 'If it hadn't been found, there would have been no Artful Dodge.'

'It had to be found, of course!' said James, looking as if he should have thought of it himself, and was mad because he hadn't.

I looked at Beans, and shrugged.

Casey spelled it out for us. 'The way the Dodger crimes work is by a "Dodge" causing confusion at the time the crime is being committed, or just afterwards. The stuff that was found in the cement wasn't really meant to put Deeny in prison. The idea was to send the police on a false trail for a short while, probably while the real criminal made his escape. To do that, it had to be discovered *at the right time*. But it couldn't be made too obvious, because if it was discovered *before* it was supposed to be . . . before one o'clock . . . it wouldn't have worked. The only safe thing the Dodger could do was to bury the cheap stuff where no one would find it, and then have someone make sure that the police *did* find it.'

'Quirke could have told them.'

'That would have meant drawing attention to himself. Quirke kept well away while the crime was being committed. He didn't want to be involved at all. There had to be a *third* person at the Lower Hall at two o'clock, when the real crime was discovered, to put the police on to the fake one. My bet is that we are up against at least a three-handed team; Quirke, the thief who stole the antiques, and a third person who made sure the "Artful Dodge" was discovered.'

'Who dunnit?' I demanded.

Which is how we all came to be back in the hall, with Casey chatting politely to PC Gray. He came away with a huge grin on his face.

'Mr Cameron of Cameron Antiques spotted it,' said Casey.

'Which makes Rat-Face suspect Number One!' I said, and I added his name to the list in my notebook. I was having to add everything in pencil because of Beans busting my carrot pen, which was a bit of a nuisance.

'I think we should pay the Cameron Antiques stall a visit,' Casey said.

'How much is this, please?' I said, holding up an old doll with a china face.

'Put that down!' the rat-faced guy howled. We knew he was Mr Cameron, but he didn't know he was Mystery Squad Suspect Number One . . . the third man in the Artful Dodger Gang.

'It's only a rotten old doll,' I said, and I waited for him to explode.'

The whole idea was for the Squad to play an Artful Dodge on him, by getting him to lose his temper with me, whilst the other three had a look around the stall for clues. That's what Casey said anyway, but nobody seemed to know what clues we were looking for!

'Put it down!' said Mr Cameron.

I put it down, hard!

He howled.

'I've got fifty pence to spend,' I said.

'Get off!' he said.

'But . . .'

'Clear off out of it. Kids!'

'My sister likes dolls. She got one for Christmas.'

He blew up like a balloon. Then he spotted Beans, who was looking inside his mummy case.

'You!' he shouted, turning round to her.

'Yes?' said Beans.

'Keep away from that. It's very delicate.'

'Sorry,' said Beans, giving him her polite little girl smile.

It was great. Meanwhile Casey and James were

having all the time they wanted to check round the stall.

'Anything helpful?' Casey asked James, as they moved away from the stall.

James shook his head.

'Me neither,' said Casey. 'Looks as if we're against a classic Locked Room Mystery, with complications.'

'What *is* a Locked Room Mystery?' Beans asked.

You'd think even Beans would know that, wouldn't you? I had to explain it to her. I know a lot about these things through my TSM research into other detectives' methods.

'A Locked Room Mystery is where you have a body discovered in a room. The room has several entrances, but all of them are locked or bolted *on the inside!*'

'We haven't got a body!' Beans said, and then she grinned and added. 'Only the mouldy old mummy!'

'Shut up, Beans,' I said, politely. 'I haven't finished explaining about Locked Room Mysteries. You have to prove who committed the crime and how it was done. How did the person get into the room when the doors were bolted on the inside, and how did they manage to bolt the door on the inside after they got out again? Something like that. Everyone knows that's a Locked Room Mystery.'

'In this case,' said James, 'the main door was locked and the two side doors bolted on the inside.'

'Be great if we could solve it,' said Casey. 'Locked Room Mysteries are special.'

'Another triumph for the Mystery Squad,' I said. *'Mystery Squad Solve Locked Room Mystery,* by our Crime Reporter, Bodger Bacon. *Police Chief Admits he was Baffled.'*

'I don't think dad would be too pleased to read that,' said Casey.

'You're forgetting something,' said Beans.

'What?'

'You haven't *solved* the Locked Room Mystery yet!'

She was right. We went down to the end of the room, and I drew a map of the Lower Hall marking all the exits and we looked at it, to see if we could get any clues.

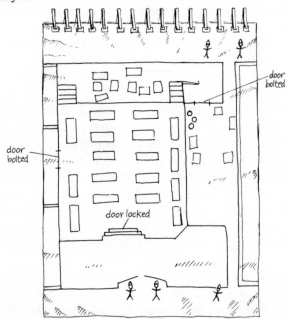

door
bolted

door
bolted

door locked

'Three doors. The two side doors were bolted, and the main door locked, after the bolting had been done,' said James. 'That was shortly after one o'clock, when the Fair closed for lunch. At ten past one the policeman guarding the main door admitted Deeny Feeney to sweep the floor. He was out again by a quarter past. He was searched, but nothing was found.'

'Deeny Feeney could have unbolted one of the doors, allowing someone else to nip inside the Lower Hall,' suggested Beans.

'Making Deeny the *fourth* member of the gang?'

Nobody thought much of that.

'He mightn't be a proper member of the gang. Maybe Quirke and Cameron and the other one just *used* him this time,' said Casey.

'I bet he was pleased when they had him arrested afterwards!' Beans said.

'Perhaps he was, Beans,' said James. 'Making Deeny look as if he was guilty of a fake crime would probably make the police less suspicious that he was involved in a real one!'

'So we think Deeny Feeney unbolted one of the doors when he was cleaning up the hall, and the crime was committed by someone who came in from outside during that period and stole the stuff . . .'

'And went out again, after which Deeny bolted the door behind him,' I finished.

'Or *her*,' said Beans.

Casey looked at James. 'Well?' he said.

'No time,' said James. 'This relies on Deeny unbolting the door to let the thief in and bolting it again after the thief had finished. Deeny was only in the room for five minutes. The thief would have had only two or three minutes to collect a large quantity of valuable antiques and get clear with it . . .'

'Which means it doesn't work!' said Casey. 'That wouldn't be possible.'

'That rules out the Deeny Feeney theory,' I said, crossing out Deeny's name.

'Not entirely,' said James. 'Deeny could have let the thief *in* by unbolting the door, or *out* by rebolting it behind the thief. He couldn't do both, that's all.'

'And my dad had policemen posted all round the building,' Casey said, and he pointed out the positions on the map.

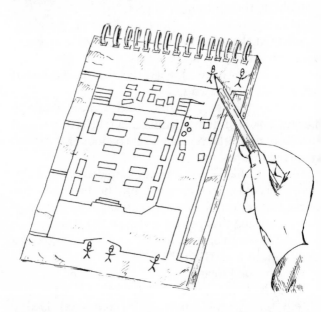

'A Classic Locked Room Mystery! The criminal has to get in, commit the crime, and get out.'

'Or stay inside!' said Beans suddenly.

'What?'

'Suppose the thief was inside the Lower Hall when the police closed it at one, inside it when Deeny came in and did his cleaning, and inside it when Deeny left. Suppose he stayed inside when the hall was re-opened?'

'Hidden, you mean?' I said.

'Come off it, Beans,' said Casey. 'My dad's men searched everything, and everybody! They looked round the Lower Hall after it was closed, *and* just after it was re-opened.'

'I bet they saw him,' said Beans, and then she added 'or *her*!' and laughed like a maniac gorilla. We didn't know what she was on about. "Or her" is a thing Beans says all the time, because she doesn't see why boys should get all the good bits.

'She's off her nut!' said Casey.

'I'm not,' said Beans. 'I know I'm not. Somebody . . . s-o-m-e—B-O-D-Y . . . was in the Lower Hall, all the time!'

Where was the thief hidden?

In the Bacon Box? Turn to **60**.

In one of the large vases? Turn to **32**.

In the mummy case? Turn to **19**.

Under one of the stalls? Turn to **6**.

If you need a clue, turn to **38**.

69

You've been custard pied . . . No one knows who the Dodger is. Turn to **28**.

70

A wooden Tent for All Weather Operations? The all-weather rain would come in through the holes! Turn to **13** and think again.

71

Turn to **55** and think again.

72

Wrong. Turn to **62** and think again.

The Mystery Squad Detective Rating

This chart will show you the Detective Rating you've earned by completing this Solve it Yourself Mystery.

You should be able to improve your score as you tackle further mysteries in the series and pick up more tips from them. Keep a note of your scores for future reference.

Your Score	*Detective Rating*
60-70	Sherlock Holmes!
50-59	Super Sleuth!
40-49	Ace Detective
30-39	Detective—1st Class
20-29	Detective—2nd Class
11-19	Junior Detective
6-10	Trainee
0-5	Beginner

If you've enjoyed reading this Solve it Yourself Mystery and would like to test your detective skills further, here are some more titles in the same series:

The Mystery Squad and the Dead Man's Message
The Mystery Squad and Mr Midnight
The Mystery Squad and the Whistling Teeth